Published in the United States, Great Britain, Canada, Australia and New Zealand
in 1991 by North-South Books, an imprint of Nord-Süd Verlag AG.
First paperback edition published in 1995.

Distributed in the United States by North-South Books, Inc., New York

Library of Congress Cataloging-in-Publication Data
Wilkoń, Piotr.
[Katzenausflug. English]
The Brave Little Kittens / by Piotr Wilkoń;
illustrated by Józef Wilkoń, translated by Helen Graves.
Translation of: Katzenausflug.
Summary: Three little kittens go outdoors for the first time
and enjoy scaring away all the animals they meet until a fierce dog appears.
[1. Cats—Fiction.   2. Animals—Fiction]   I. Wilkoń, Józef. Ill.   II. Title.
PZ7.W6543Br 1991
[E]—dc20 90-44095

British Library Cataloguing in Publication Data
Wilkoń, Piotr
The Brave Little Kittens.
I. Title   II. Wilkoń, Józef   III. Katzenausflug.
English
833.914 [J]

ISBN 1-55858-503-6 (paperback)
1 3 5 7 9 10 8 6 4 2
Printed in Belgium

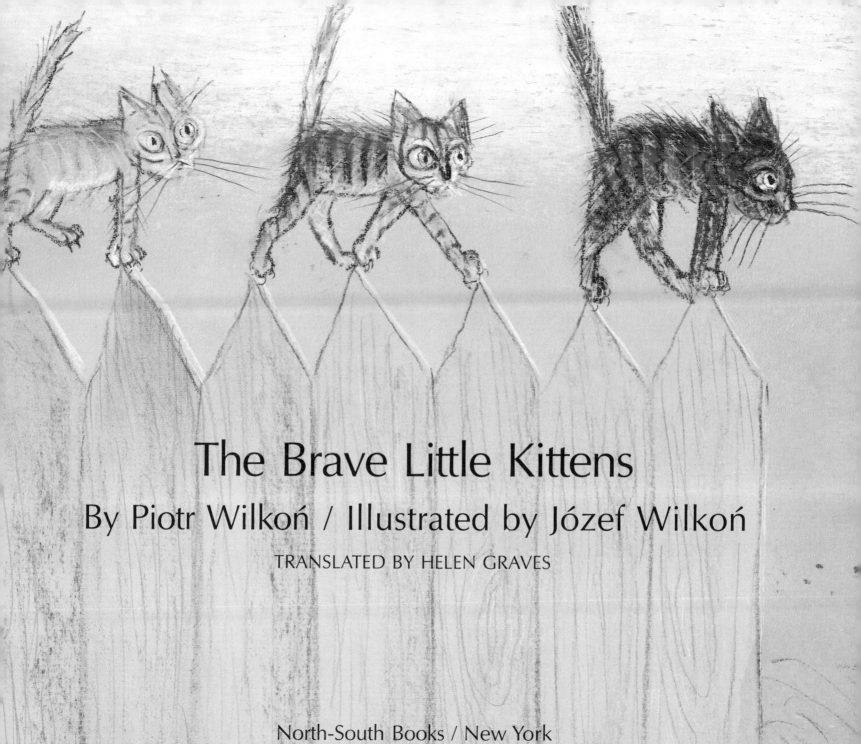

The Brave Little Kittens

By Piotr Wilkoń / Illustrated by Józef Wilkoń

TRANSLATED BY HELEN GRAVES

North-South Books / New York

Mama Cat had three beautiful kittens: two boys, Tim and Tom, and a girl named Tot. Tim was the darkest of the three. His fur was mostly black and dark gray. Tom looked exactly like his mother. Tot was the smallest and her fur was light gray with touches of white.

The kittens played indoors all day long. They scampered around, getting their exercise by batting everything that moved with their paws. Sometimes, Tim and Tom would wrestle on the floor. The kittens even chased their own little tails!

Once, they saw a spider and rushed right after it. But the spider climbed up the wall where the kittens couldn't get at it. They watched with shining eyes as the spider slunk away.

Then one day Mama Cat said, "No more child's play! Today you can go outside. It's time for you to grow up and learn the things every kitten needs to know."

CHAPTER 1

The first time the kittens walked outside they were blinded by the bright sunlight. But that didn't last long. Soon they felt completely at ease in the open air.

There was so much to see! The kittens romped madly from one thing to the next, smelling the strange new plants and digging their claws into the trunks of trees.

Before too long they came across a dragonfly, buzzing close to the ground. Tim ran to it and made a mighty leap, but the dragonfly flew across the yard to the barn.

The three kittens ran after it.

It was dark and dusty inside the barn. The dragonfly had disappeared, but pretty soon they spotted a mouse. They crouched down low and very slowly crept around a haystack. They leaped after the mouse and chased it all around the barn until it disappeared into a little hole in the wall.

Next they went to the chicken coop, where a hen was scratching in the dirt. The kittens watched the strange-looking animal for a few minutes.

"Let's go over and say hello," said Tom.

But when the kittens got close, the hen cackled loudly, beat its wings wildly, and fluttered up to the top of a fence post.

"It's fun to play outdoors!" said Tot.

"Especially when everyone is afraid of us!" added Tim. "Come on, let's explore the field."

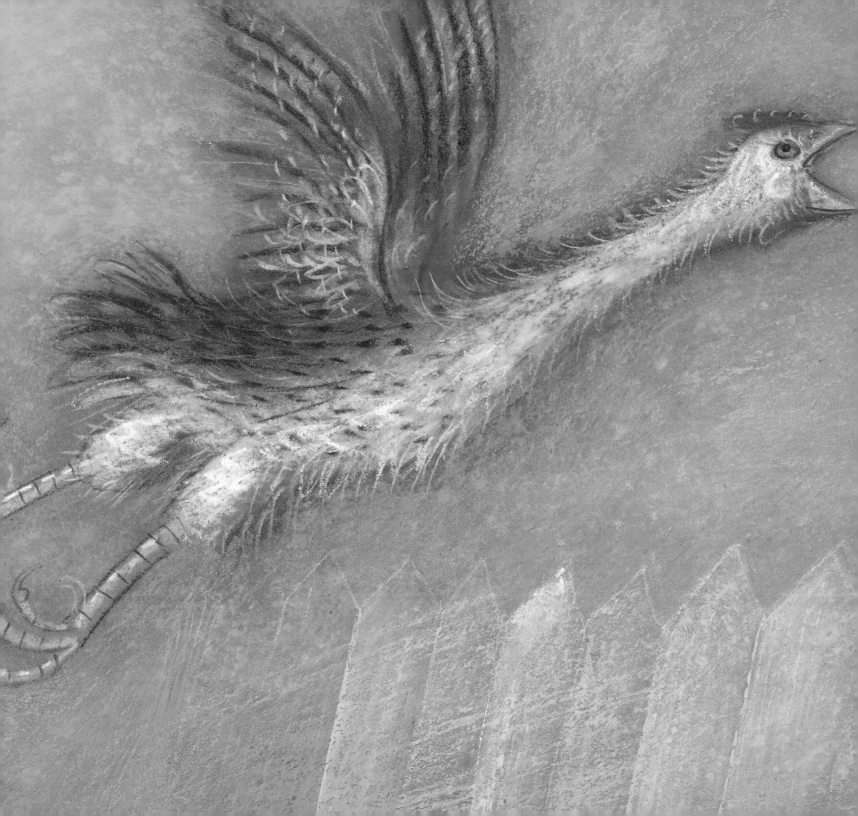

The grass in the field was tall and cool.

As they walked along they came upon an animal with tall pink ears crouched in the grass ahead of them. The kittens froze and stared at the rabbit, but suddenly it leaped into the air and hopped away.

"After it!" shouted Tot.

They dashed across the field, running faster and faster.
They were having so much fun, but suddenly...

. . . right there in front of them was a fierce animal with sharp white teeth!

The three little kittens arched their backs and hissed at the dog.

The dog crouched down and barked at the kittens.

The kittens turned around and ran as fast as they could,
with the barking dog close behind.

"Mama! Mama! Help! Help!" they yelled.

Mama Cat appeared in an instant, arching her back and hissing loudly.

The dog yelped at her a few times, but soon he turned and walked away.

"Where have you been?" asked Mama Cat. "I've been looking everywhere for you."

"We've been exploring!" said Tim.

"We were chasing animals!" said Tom.

"We were having fun until we met that dog," said Tot.

"You're brave little kittens," said Mama Cat softly. "But you must learn to be careful. Not everyone you meet will be scared of you."

When they returned to the house, the three little kittens
snuggled up to their mother. It had been an exhausting day, and
soon everyone but Tim was asleep.

Tim lay awake a little while longer. He couldn't stop thinking
about everything that had happened and about the new
adventures the next day would bring.